THE MURDERS IN LEATHER TOWN

BY DAVID EVANS

TABLE OF CONTENTS

Three years ago, there were a few horrific murders that had occurred in the community of Leather Town. Leather Town has a small population of approximately one thousand people. For the most part, the folks in Town are kind and friendly to the travelers as they pass through their town. Downtown there are two diners that serve breakfast and dinner every day.

There was a bad rain storm that flooded out one of the grocery stores and while the grocery store was being cleaned up, a man walked in wearing a hoodie and pulled out a gun and started shooting up the place.

The several volunteers and the people working in the store took cover, luckily one of the volunteers was an off duty Police officer who immediately went into action.

He took his gun out and fired at the man hitting him in the leg, he collapsed and the officer tied his hands together with a tie down that someone gave to him.

While the suspect was tied down another person called the Police, several minutes later the Police showed up and took him away. On the outskirts of town, there's a lumber company called "Herman Logging."

This company was founded in 1885 by a wealthy man, who's name is . Ethan. One day one of the workers didn't show up for work, the boss called the man's home phone but there was no answer.

He immediately called the Police, they went out to his house but he wasn't there, no one knows what happened to him. One week ago the Police were called out to an active logging site, when they got there 2 loggers were hiding in their trucks. The officer walked over to the truck and the man rolled down the window.

"Can you fellas describe to me what happened here?"

"Yes"

We were having our lunch break, and heard yells coming from our bosses trailer. As we were running towards the trailer, we saw 2 guys with chainsaws with blood all over them retreating back into the woods. I froze in fear, while my buddy pulled out his pistol and started shooting at them.

I quickly made a run for it back to my truck, once back in my truck I locked the doors. I wasn't going to leave my friend behind, so I waited for him to come back before taking off out of there. My friend said that when he found his boss he was in pieces, with blood splattered all over the walls.

"Do you fellas know anyone who would do that?"

"No"

Neither one of us are going to come to work tomorrow, unless there's a security guard with us.

"How long have you fellas been working here?"

"2 years."

Hold on I'm getting a phone call, he quickly answered his phone. Hello, it's your Aunt Jacky you need to come see this. I'm currently in the middle of an interview, I'll be out when it's over.

I'm afraid for my life, then get out of there. I don't want to go outside of my house, just sit tight I'll be there soon. I love you bye, that was my dog sitter calling. She told me that she couldn't come out tomorrow to watch my dogs. I'm going to ask you both two more questions then you may go.

"Do you think these two men stole the chainsaws?"

"No," we don't.

Their chainsaws look different than ours do, we definitely weren't going to ask them where they got their chainsaws from.

"Could you see their faces?"

"No," they had masks on.

I'm going to ask the both of you not to come to work for two days, that's alright with us. It's been nice talking with you officer but I have to go, if you have any more questions here's my phone number. He started his truck, and they drove down the path. Several deer crossed the path in front of them, slow down you almost hit those deer.

> "When are you going to get a truck of your own?"

> "In 3 days."

I know what you're going to ask me next.

> "Are you going to drop me off at my house before going to your Aunts?"

> "No," you'll have to wait.

Just play on your phone until I'm done at my aunt's, I'm sure that you have many people to text. I could text my girlfriend, then go ahead and do that. You better speed up, don't look over or you're going to crash.

> "Who was it?"

> "The two men with the chainsaws."

You should have just pulled your gun out and shot them, you just let fear come over you. I can't believe that you're turning around, if they come after us now I'm going to run them over. I don't understand you, you were terrified of them the other day and just wanted to get away from them now it's a whole new story.

I'm going to try talking to them, I don't think it's a good idea. His friend pointed the men out to him, they probably won't hear you talking to them because they're further in the woods now. Excuse me guys I need to have a word with you both, the both men began walking towards them. They fired up their chainsaws, and were closing in on them.

Unless you have a death wish, we better make tracks out of here. Hello I'm speaking to the both of you, you can answer me anytime now. They quickly sped off, you let them get too close to us. He spun the truck around and went straight towards them, the men holding the chainsaws retreated back behind a tree.

You barely missed that tree, your putting both of our lives in danger. He looked over and saw the chainsaw blade cutting through his friends neck, blood splattered on the other mans face. He sped off out of there, and didn't look back. He didn't stop until he got to his Aunts house, as he was pulling in he saw a dead lying there.

He looked over at his friend, and he was missing his head. He got out of his truck and walked to the front door and opened it and entered, his aunt was shaking and she immediately saw the blood and asked what had happened, he said that he was in an accident and she said that's my neighbors body out there.

He talked with his Aunt awhile to try and comfort her, before leaving he handed his friends gun to her, and told her to use it on the murderer if he came back. He gave her a hug, then he exited her place and walked back to his truck and got in and drove out of there. Once he got home, he took a shovel out of his shed and dug a hole and buried his friend.

Some time ago there was an incident that occurred at the water tower, a fugitive had escaped and climbed to the top of the tower. Once at the top of the tower, he took the rifle off of his shoulder, and began firing at people and cars going by. This went on for several agonizing minutes, the remaining people on the streets entered buildings to take cover.

One of the people called 911, and within several minutes the Police showed up. They completely surrounded the tower, soon afterwards a Police helicopter flew in. Even the swat team showed up, one of the officers we're ready to climb up the ladder to go after the suspect.

Another officer tapped him on his shoulder, allow the swat team to take over. Don't argue with me just step away from the ladder, and the officer walked away.

One of the swat team members, brought out a loudspeaker from the swat truck. Come down from that tower at once, or were going to shoot you with non-lethal bullets.

The man still didn't make a move, one of the swat officers fired at him. The sand bags struck him in the torso, the suspect lost his balance and plummeted to his death. The coroner was called to the scene and took the body away, the suspects family were given a call but were away on vacation.

In Leathertown, there's a small museum. Sometimes the elders and kids go to see the exhibits featured in the museum, a month ago someone placed a bomb in the lobby of the museum, and set it off when the place was full of people.

48 people lost there lives, and 4 were wounded. Since then, the museum installed several more cameras, and metal detectors. Recently the museum held a painting contest, that lasted for three days.

It's never opens on the weekend, and it's free for kids to go to the museum. The children of the town go to the museum during the holidays for special events. There's a water park that's 2 hours away from the town and in the summertime, that's where the kids of the town spend their time.

The towns local school is called Leather East High School, It's a small Schoolhouse, In 1959 there was a horrific massacre. 39 people were killed and 11 wounded, the attacker was a student who was given a machine gun for his birthday. In 1990, he died in prison after having a heart attack.

While on the second floor that's where they store their extra books and such. The Schoolhouse has many large windows to allow the students to get a good look at what's going on outside.

The county Commissioner wants to shut down the local beer distributor because he has reason to believe that the owner is selling drugs and overcharging his customers for a case of beer.

The town commissioner is a little man who has a big attitude and wants everything done his way, he's lived in town for 2 years now and used to live in Arizona. He drives around the town in his new truck, everyone else in town drives older vehicles.

One day when the commissioner was driving to his office, a truck was following behind him. He sped up, in hopes of the losing truck behind him. He made a few random turns, he looked in his rearview mirror and they were still there. He thought to himself should I pull over? But decided not to stop.

He was driving down a desolate road, road crews were doing work on the shoulder of the road. Off to his right was a grassy field, he placed his truck into four wheel drive and drove off onto the field. Up ahead he saw a trail that led through the woods, now the guy behind him was further away from him.

He held onto the wheel with one hand while using the other hand to bring out his cell phone from his coat pocket. He was already to make a call when he noticed that his phone was out of battery, and angrily threw it down.

He went on a ways down the trail, passing by a farm. Somehow the other driver was still behind him, some gravel flew up hitting the truck behind him. He saw a sign that said the road ends here, but he was going too fast to stop.

He drove through the sign, and his truck went down a steep embankment. The other driver wasn't daring enough to go down the steep incline, and left him alone. It took him a while to find his way back onto a road, once back on the road he made his way back to his office.

In the town, there's a sheriff but no deputy. The sheriff has 7 Police officers who work under him. The officers are very respectful towards the sheriff, the sheriff's name is Javier and his deputies name was Ross. The deputy had passed away rather mysteriously.

Nobody knows exactly how he died or what happened, the sheriff couldn't believe that his deputy had died. The sheriff was told that his deputy had been murdered. The other officers couldn't tell him the story and didn't care for the deputy. There's still a picture hanging up in the sheriff's office of the deputy.

His deputy was a young fellow in his late thirties, and it was sad that he died so young. While the sheriff is 43 years old and gets around well. He's never had any health problems to speak of, each morning when he gets up he drinks one raw egg and then makes a scrambled egg for his German Shepard.

He's a rather lonely man that just lives for his job and that's all he really worries about these days. 2 years ago, his wife had divorced him. She said that he was too controlling and never did what she wanted to do, so she left him rather quickly.

Her name was Martha, and she was one year younger than him. All throughout his life he had a dog, he says that loves his dog better than some of his friends. He's not too social and likes to sit in his old rocking chair and whittle away at a piece of wood.

The sheriff shows up at his office at 5:00 in the morning and he says that he likes to do that to get some extra work done and to keep his desk well organized.

He likes his office to remain quiet so that he can focus, his deputy used to show up at 7:00 in the morning and turn on the coffee maker and get things going for the day.

He misses how his deputy would help him out with finding a suspect, now it's just him and an women who answers the phones and files paperwork. The woman looked miserable every day that she shows up for work and doesn't smile until it's time for her to go home for the day.

She likes to eat her candy and let the wrapper lay there on her desk, which drives the sheriff crazy. He also says to her if you make a mess then you will be responsible for cleaning it up.

She shakes her head in disgust when he talks to her, but can't fire her because she's the commissioner's grandmother. The commissioner is a rather controlling man who's never happy until he's controlling someone else. He told the sheriff that if he fires his grandmother, then he'll get him demoted and make him work as a deputy instead of the sheriff.

The sheriff keeps well enough alone and doesn't argue with the commissioner or come in contact with him very often. It's been a 1 since he saw the commissioner and hopes that it will be another until he sees the commissioner. The sheriff attended a technical school for investigative work, right after High School.

He attended the technical school for 4 years and enjoyed the class he had attended, he had mentioned to his classmates that he was going to become the sheriff of the town.

Nobody believed that he would be able to fulfill such a serious job as being sheriff, but he proved them all wrong and went on with learning about investigative work.

He would get the best grades out of all of the other classmates. Javier keeps his desk well organized. All the drawers in his desk, are filled with something. He keeps his pens and pencils in the top drawer and the white out in the next drawer down.

On the corner of his desk is a picture of his beloved dog, this picture was taken a year ago, he remembers this day like it was yesterday. He likes to play fetch with his dog everyday.

Through the years, he has had 2 dogs that he cherished so much. Javier can still remember when him and Ross used to go out and investigate crime scenes.

He would enjoy talking to Ross about guns and cars. Ross liked to collect rare silver coins, the day he died his collection was given over to his young son who was 18 years old at the time.

His son is now 25 years old, his son really misses his dad and thinks of him every day. Twice a week he goes to his dad's gravestone and puts a bouquet of roses on the gravestone and says a prayer.

He says several prayers then leaves the graveyard after several minutes and goes to see his grandmother afterwards, who always has a smile on her face and embraces him with a hug

He loves his grandmother who's 84 years old and is on oxygen and has a lot of difficulties getting around as she ages. She walks around with a cane to keep her balance, every other month his mother has to go to the Dr. to check her lungs and heart.

Ross had loved his son so much that he would spend 2 hours after work and play a game of catch with his son. Not much was known about his mother, who was an estranged woman.

Leather town hasn't been a very safe place throughout the years, most of the people in town go to church every Sunday and show up at the church at 9:00 in the morning.

The town folk isn't all religious and just a few outliers remain living on the outskirts of town, these particular people are narcissistic and believe there's no God.

They keep their houses dark inside and light very rarely passes into their houses. In the town, there are 2 bus stations. That's busy each day taking people to the places they want to go to, it costs the riders of the buses, $1.00 to ride the bus.

The folks who ride the bus don't have cars and don't like to pay for any extras. All of the buses are old and need to be replaced, the buses were built in the 1990's. Congress will soon introduce a infrastructure bill to have the busses replaced with new ones.

They're slow and a lot of fumes fill the sky from their old engines. The buses are owned by the local bus company, the company's owner is a little man who doesn't know much about business.

Chapter 1: The First Incident

One time one of the buses broke down just outside of Leather town, and the tow truck that was called out, didn't have the right equipment so another larger tow truck had to be dispatched. The bus was full of overlly anxious people.

Some of the people were complaining that they were going to be late to work. The bus driver got tired of hearing all of the people complaining and stepped off the bus and observed the tow truck driver getting the bus ready to be towed.

The tow truck driver was struggling to get the tie downs out of his truck, all the tie downs were twisted and there was a kink in them. It took the tow truck driver a few minutes to get the tie downs apart and ready to wrap around the back of the bus.

One of the passengers on the bus got up and closed the door, she sat down and stared out the window at the bus driver. She gave the bus driver a dirty look like she was disgusted with him. He just looked away from her and continued to watch what the tow truck driver was doing. The bus driver's name was Marshall.

He's been driving this same bus for 2 years and this is the first time that the bus had ever broken down. The bus was broken down on an back road with the woods on either sides of them. There was plenty of wildlife to be seen, like deer and turkey and the occasional squirrel that was daring enough to cross the road.

Most of the people on the bus pulled out their smartphone and were listening to music and weren't paying attention to anything that was going on around them. Several yards away a doe and her baby crossed the road, the doe quickly took her baby with her into the woods and wasn't seen again.

"What's your name?"

"My name is Virgil"

"What's your name?"

"My name's Marshall, it's nice to have met you, likewise."

"Do you need some help with those tie-downs?"

"No," thanks, I got them.

"How old are those tie-downs?"

"They're several years old."

I want to buy a new pair of tow ropes and an extra set of tie-downs.

"How many people have you towed today?"

"3"

Tomorrow I will have to tow out 2 people.

"What happened to their vehicles?"

"They're stuck in their own driveway."

Their driveways were too icy, and their vehicles must have slid down into a snowbank.

"Are the vehicles cars or trucks?"

"I don't know."

"Do you get paid well for everything that you do?"

"Yes,"

I'm just happy to have a job, to be honest with you. I haven't had a job for 2 months.

"May I ask why?"

"I got hurt on the job."

I was walking along, and I didn't care to look down and I walked over a patch of ice and I fell on my back and twisted my left hip. That must have hurt a lot.

"Did you have to go for Physical Therapy?"

"Yes, for 3 weeks, and every time that I did the stretches I was in bad pain."

"How was the Therapist?"

"She was an old lady that wouldn't smile and thought that she was funny."

She would tell some jokes, they weren't funny and I pretended to laugh, then she would make a frown face at me. She was miserable every time that I was with her.

"How long did you have to stay at the Physical Therapy place?"

"I had to stay there for two hours, I was glad to get back home."

I need to get these tow chains around the frame of the bus, I understand. I have a job to do, not talk about the boring days that I had to spend in therapy because of my own fault. I think that the bus is blocking the road too much.

No, it will be okay but thanks for your concern, a car went past the bus. I'm afraid that someone's going to come racing around the corner and crash into the back of the bus. I've placed the emergency flares at the corner and a few feet from the bus, everyone will see the flares and slow down.

"Are you sure I cannot give you a hand?"

"Yes,"

Unless you want to crawl under the bus and hook up the tow chains to the frame. I would be doing your job, that's true, but I won't tell my shop that you helped me.

"Do you want to crawl under the bus?"

"No," then I'll do it.

"Is there anything else that I can do?"

"No," not at the moment.

"Do you hear that revving sound?"

"Yes," I do, I don't know where it's coming from.

I wouldn't be concerned about the noise, so now I'm going to crawl under the bus and get started. There's 2 men holding chainsaws walking down the street with masks on.

They keep on revving up there chainsaw engines and I think they have murderess intentions, I don't know what to do, I'm scared out of my witts. I'm afraid of what may happen next.

> "What do you have that could deter the men?"

> "I have pepper spray and I don't have a gun."

> "We need to do something now?

> "How close are the men now?"

> "They're 85 feet away and keep walking towards us, they're walking slowing and keep revving there chainsaws."

I can see they're wearing aprons with blood all over them and there's blood all over the blades of the chainsaws, the people on the bus weren't paying attention to what was going on and soon would be absolutely terrified.

I'm so scared that I want to run away from here. No, don't do that, you won't make it. Yes, I will. You're safe, under the bus but I'm not, I can't stop shaking.

Marshal tried to get on the bus and hide in there along with the rest of the people. Yes, but I'm in charge of the lives of all the people on the bus. Do something to stop the crazy men, I can't fight against them because they have chainsaws and I think they will cut us all up.

"What's the 1 man doing now?"

"He just paused for a moment and went into the woods?"

"Is he still in the woods?"

"Yes," and he's still walking in our direction.

"Can you still hear the chainsaw?"

"Yes," and now he's revving the engine again.

I think he's cutting down some trees, but I can't be sure. I think the 1 man is going to cut down some trees to block the road so that we cannot get past.

"What else would he be doing in the woods besides cutting down the trees?"

"Good question."

"I don't think these men have any friends or pets, that visit them in the woods."

"What are you doing at the front of the bus?"

"I'm trying to get back on my bus."

"What's the matter?"

"I can't get back inside the bus."

"Someone must have closed the door not knowing that the door would have locked."

"What are you going to do about the locked door?"

"I'm going to bang on the buses window and see if someone can open the door."

"Do you still see both men?"

"No," but I still hear the chainsaw revving.

Look out, a huge tree came down over the road in front of them. I tell you what, why don't you get under the bus with me and hide from the men with the chainsaws? I think I'll join you, Marshall quickly slid under the bus and got dirt all over the back of the shirt, I'm so scared and can't myself to calm down.

"How long are we going to stay under here?"

"Until the one twin goes away."

I want to stop the men, why because I don't want to see anyone else get killed. Yes, but if you go after them then you will be the one who gets killed. They would chop you up so quickly you wouldn't have a chance to fight, 1 dead person is better than a few.

"Why haven't you called the Police yet?"

"Because I can't get any cell reception out here."

"Why don't you try your phone?"

"I can't I left it on the bus."

Suddenly the people on the bus began to scream out.

"What?"

"Both men just came walking out of the woods and are now standing in the front of the bus and are revving up there chainsaws."

Screams erupted from the bus and the bus began to shift back and forth while the people began to freak out.

"Why don't you sneak over to your truck and run over both men?"

"No," they would see me and I wouldn't do that.

I don't want to harm them, if you don't then I will. I don't want you going out there either.

"Do you think the crazy men know that were under here?"

"No," but we should speak in a quiet tone to one another.

Whatever you say we will do, suddenly screams erupted from the bus

"What do you think's happening now?"

"The both men are probably trying to find a way to get into the bus to attack the people."

Then a car passed by and the driver sped off when he saw the crazy men.

"Do you still have the pepper spray?"

"No," it's in my truck

Were really in a tight spot, Yes, we are. I'm afraid that we won't be able to get out of here and I'll never see my kids again. I didn't realize that you had kids. Yes, and they mean the world to me. The screaming increased and didn't stop, I no longer see the feet of the men, then they must have gotten into the bus.

"Did you hear that?"

"Yes," it sounded like a car pulling up.

I hope it's the Police, I don't think so

"Who would have called the Police?"

"That motorist that drove by, I doubt he would have called the Police, let's agree to disagree on that."

The screams and yells continued, and they couldn't hear the revving of the chainsaw. After 20 minutes the screaming stopped, and the chainsaws were still idling

I'm afraid that both men killed all of the people on the bus, I think so and it was my duty to protect the people. I wouldn't worry about that right now, you've done all you can to help yourself.

"What are the people's parents and friends going to say about their deaths?"

"You think too far into things."

"Just stop it and allow me to think about what were going to do."

"Did you just hear a man's voice?"

"Yes," please stop yelling into my ears.

"I'm lying here right next to you remember?"

"Yes," I do

Chapter 2: Shock

Someone else approached the bus, both men immediately revved up there chainsaws. They heard the man shout, I'm a Police officer and you're both under arrest. Now take your chainsaws and put them down, come out with both your hands up, or I'll shoot. 2 shots rang out while the chainsaws stayed idling.

They heard the officer say Sir, I told you I was going to shoot. You didn't stop, so I had to shoot you both. I'm going to call this in, I can't believe what I'm looking at. The men continued to listen to what the officer was saying.

Hi, dispatch this is officer Rudy and I'm reporting a horrific crime. Go ahead, I'm standing by a large bus that seems to have broken down. All of the people in the bus were murdered by the twins with chainsaws.

I have to report that I had to shoot both men with chainsaws, I had to shoot the both men in self-defense. The men just got back up, and they're going back into the woods.

"That's all right officer Rudy as long as you are all right"

"How many shots have you fired?"

"I had to shoot the both men twice in the chest"

"Were the suspects wearing any type of body armor?"

"Yes," and they were wearing bloody aprons.

They had masks on there faces, and I don't know where they came from and I don't have a positive ID on them at the moment. They said to one another I think we should take a break, no I disagree with you.

"Why?"

"I just have a bad gut feeling about it."

"What are you afraid of?"

"I'm afraid that there's another man waiting out there to come and attack again."

I can't believe that you're thinking that right now, suddenly they heard the officer screaming and he stopped talking and once again they heard another chainsaw being revved.

Then they heard another gunshot ring out and then there was dead silence. See that my gut feeling was correct. Yes, you were right this time.

"Can you see anything going on out there?"

"Yes"

All I can see is the officer lying down on the ground and another set of feet a few feet away from the bus.

"Does the Police officer look like he's breathing?"

"No," there's a puddle of blood around his motionless body.

It appears that the both men cut off both of the officer's arms and his leg, that's absolutely horrific.

"What's the other man doing now?"

"It's hard for me to tell, he's just walking around looking at the bus and the dead officer."

We need to talk quietly, so that the men don't hear us. I thought we were talking quite enough; we are now.

"Any new movement of the one man?"

"No"

He just keeps on holding onto the chainsaw and revving it.

"I thought you said the one man cut down a tree blocking the road?"

"Yes," he did but somehow people are getting past the tree.

It appears to me that the one man is walking away from the bus and towards the Police car.

"What do you think he's looking for in the Police car?"

"I'm not so sure about what he's looking for, let me think a moment about that."

I looked at my watch and an hour has passed by so far, then you must be a time watcher.

"Do you think the men can talk?"

"Yes"

I leaned out further and I saw the man's face in the mirror, his face is all tore up. I hope I never see his face again, I hope you're right. I'm getting cold out here, me too, it feels like it's 20 degrees out here and the wind's blowing.

There's blood running down the street towards us, I hate the sight of blood. Just don't look at it, all I can smell is death out here, I know, but I know we can get through this situation. See that your positivity is showing through.

"What's the one man doing now?"

"He's cutting off the doors to the "Police car, and he just slipped on the blood that was on the ground in front of him."

He dropped the chainsaw on the ground and left it there, He's now trying to climb into the Police car. No, he's sitting in the driver seat, oh gross he just licked the steering wheel. This man is disgusting, and I can't stand it for much longer. Instead of keep on asking me what the man is doing.

"Why don't you take a look for yourself?"

"The position I currently am in I can't see much."

I understand, I have a pounding headache, my stress level is through the roof and I can't stop shaking. Just try to think happy thoughts and the time will pass by.

"Do you think that the men know how to drive?"

"No."

The man just climbed back out of the car and picked up his chainsaw again.

"I'm hoping that someone takes his chainsaw "

"Do you think someone will?"

"No"

The one man is chasing after the dog and is trying to cut him into pieces. That poor dog, I wish we could save that poor dog. Now the dog is running over this way in our direction.

Dog please don't come over and alert the men that we're under here, it's no use the dog is already over here trying to get to us. Then they saw the black boots of the one man, just behind the dog.

The dog let out just yelp and the man sawed the dog's body clean in half, blood went all over him and on the side of the bus. Neither men said a word, the dog's body laid in a pool of blood by the side of the bus.

Virgil and Marshall were so scared that neither one of them could get a word out. They were staring at the body of the dead dog and couldn't believe what had just happened.

The one man took his chainsaw and turned it off and walked over to the front of the bus. The man got on the bus and it went eerily quiet, he had left the chainsaw by the side of the bus.

Marshall and Virgin were staring at the chainsaw, there was blood and guts all over the blade of the chainsaw. Blood kept running down the sides of the chainsaw, the smell of blood filled the air.

"What do you think?"

"I think that both men are real crazy killers and I hope someone stops them."

"Like whom?"

"Like another Police officer"

I can't think straight from being under this bus for all this time. I tell you what I'm going to make a run for it soon.

"How soon?"

"In ten minutes or less."

You can't stay here until nighttime, I realize that but I'm scared that the crazy men are going to get a hold of me and kill me. The man got out of the bus and walked over to his chainsaw and picked it up. He didn't start it up, and walked away from the bus and headed down the road and walked into the woods.

"What is it?"

"The men are walking away and now we can escape."

"Are you ready to get out of here?"

"Yes"

I have such a bad backache, and it hurts to move. Stop making excuses and let's get out of here. We don't have much time, I'm coming, Ouch my hand.

"What happened?"

"Virgil replied, I tripped over the dead dog."

I think I broke my right hand because I fell on it, you're moving so slowly. I tell you what, I will look for the keys to the Police car and you keep watch.

"What if the men come out of the woods?"

"Then we'll hide."

"What are you doing looking through the dead officer's pockets?"

"I'm trying to find the keys, because they aren't in the
ignition."

I finally found the keys in the top pocket of the officer's shirt, thank god.
Come on get in and let's get out of here, I'm trying to. I have a slight
limp in my leg, wait here. Please be quick, I will don't you worry. Virgil
quickly ran into the bus.

Suddenly he heard the faint sound of a chainsaw and immediately ran off
the bus and jumped in the driver seat so fast that his feet barely even
touched the ground. I never saw you move so fast before.

"What's the matter?"

"The crazy men are coming out again so let's get
going then."

Virgil spun out the back tires and now I can see both men in the rearview mirror chasing after us.

"It's okay now, were safe."

"Why didn't you try to start your truck?"

"I did and it didn't want to start."

I did that while I was looking for the key to the Police car, that was
irresponsible of you to let your truck back there.

"What else did you want me to do?"

"At least move your truck from the middle of the
road."

"Do you want to go back there then?"

"No"

That's what I thought.

"Where are we going?"

"Straight to the Police Department, but we stole their
Police car."

I don't care, we need help right now. But we might get arrested, that's
the least of my worries right now.

"How far out are we from the Police Station?"

"Just another 15 minutes and the car only has half a
tank of gas."

My right hand is really hurting me.

"Would you like it if I drove for a while?"

"No," I'm okay,

I'm holding onto the steering wheel with my left hand, that's good to see
that you have stopped shaking so much. I feel much better now, you
know you aren't doing the speed limit, and this car has no doors.

"Are you afraid that you're going to fall out of the
car?"

"Yes," I am

"Do you have your seat belt on?"

"Yes," then what are you worried about?

"I'm afraid that you are going to crash."

I may have a broken hand, but I can still steer the car just fine with my left hand. You're lucky this car isn't stick shift.

"What's with all of the people crossing the street over there?"

"It looks like some kind of street fair is going on."

"Do you like street fairs?"

"No," I don't.

There must be 20 people out in the street, I'm not worried about the people right now, I'm in so much pain. Then you need to see the Dr. no not right now. We need to get the Police after those crazy men who got away into the woods.

"Are you going to slowly pull into the parking space by the Police Station?"

"No," I'm going to drive the way I want.

"You're being a front seat driver, instead of a back-seat driver.

"Are you trying to be funny?"

"Yes," I am.

"How comes you are always frowning?"

"I'm afraid of that I won't see my family again."

You're safe now, so forget about those sad thoughts and think along with me. You know I'm afraid that you and I will be arrested for taking this Police car. I agree with you, you're thinking negatively just like me. In some ways, our personalities are the same.

It's such a nice day outside out here, the sky's blue and there's not a cloud in the sky. It's a nice day today, the slight breeze feels so good. Although it's only 30 degrees out here.

Look at the crowd of people over there by the convenience store, I'm looking, the store is probably having some kind of sale today. Look at that elderly man standing over there looking at our car. Yes, I'm watching him, he's probably never seen a Police car without its doors. The elderly man approached them.

"What happened to this car?"

"It was in an accident"

"What kind of accident?"

"The doors were sawed off"

"By whom?"

"By men with chainsaws."

"How many of them were after you?"

"2 of them."

"Do you personally know the men who were chasing
us with chainsaws?"

"Yes," I know who they are

"How do you know?"

"They were in a legend book that I read just two
weeks ago, about this towns history"

I only know that they really exist. My name is Virgil, and this is Marshall,
It's nice to have met you both. We were attacked by 2 men with
chainsaws they have been called the monstrous twins, we didn't know
that.

"What's your name Sir, my name is Clifford."

"It's nice to have met you."

"Where are the both of you headed?"

"To the Police Station"

"Are you 2 officers?"

"No," Marshall is a bus driver and I'm a tow truck driver.

"Where's your truck?"

"It's on the right side of the road just outside of town."

"Where's your bus?"

"It broke down by his truck and I parked it on the left side of the road."

Chapter 3: Clear Skies Ahead

I think I've saw you once before, you were driving the bus past here and I got on your bus twice before. I can say that you're a good driver, thank you. I'm going to let you go then, it was great talking with you, I have a question for you about the monstrous twins.

> "What's the question?"

> "Do you know where the crazy chainsaw twins live?"

> "Legend has it that they live in the middle of the woods in a small cabin, just outside of Leather town."

> "Do you know how many people they have murdered?"

> "Yes," I do

Legend has it they have killed more than 12 people who had become stranded along the roadway. That's a lot people to be killed by a chainsaw.

I pity those souls who got cut up by a chainsaw, all the pain and agony they must have gone through. I would never want to be attacked by a crazy chainsaw man. I agree with you.

> "How come nobody ever confronted them?"

> "They were probably far too terrified just to see them, then to confront them"

One of the men was shot by a Police officer and survived.

"Where did the men go then?"

"They killed the officer, then retreated into the woods."

I would love to stay here and talk with the both of you, but now I must go and get to the grocery store and get my wife some milk. Have a good rest of the day. Thanks, you guys too.

"I want you to enter the Police Station first."

"Why's that?"

"So that they question you first."

Since you told me that, I'm going to make you go in first.

"Do I have to?"

"Yes," you have no choice now.

I bet the Police saw us driving their patrol car, no I don't think so.

"Do you see any Policemen standing out here?"

"No," I don't.

Now walk me with over to the Police Station. The Police are probably going to ask us a bunch of questions but, I don't want to spend a night in jail. I don't think you will, you're over thinking things and it's only going to make you more stressed out.

"Have you ever been in the Police Station before?"

"Yes," I have and there's nothing to worry about.

"If you say so."

Allow me to open the door first, and they stepped into the Police Station. There was a Policeman sitting in a desk chair behind a desk, sorting through paperwork and missing person's reports.

"Good day officer, what may I do for you gentleman?"

"There was an accident and a life or death struggle had ensued."

"What else happened gentlemen?"

"We escaped a killer, and what's the moral of the story gentleman?"

"One of your officers came out to the scene and was killed by the monstrous twins with chainsaws."

Go on gentlemen, and my tow truck broke down and we took the Policeman's car.

"What happened to the patrol car gentleman?"

"The crazy man with the chainsaw cut off the front doors to it."

"I assume that the car is still drive-able?"

"Yes," it is Sir.

"What's your first name?"

"My name is Virgil, and this is Marshall."

"Nice to have met you both."

"What's your name officer?"

"My name is officer Floyd, and I've been on the force for 2 years so far."

"You seem like you have a lot of work to do today, yes that's right."

"Do you have a gun or carry permit?"

"No."

"What do you do for work?"

"I'm a bus driver here in Leather town."

"Have you ever been in an accident?"

"No," I do the speed limit.

I make sure not to go over the speed limit, as I'm driving. Very good I'm glad to hear that.

"Are you going to arrest us and place us in jail?"

"No," just a few more questions, then we'll see what happens next.

"I can see that your hands are trembling, you can calm down and relax."

"Have you heard about the twins with the chainsaws before?"

"Yes," there have been many reports and sightings of them

I'm surprised that the witnesses are still alive

"Where's the sheriff today?"

"He's out investigating a crime scene."

You're a very curious fellow, everyone tells me that.

"Excuse me, but where's the deputy?"

"He had died 2 years ago."

There was never a replacement hired, but Elma works here, she's the grandmother of the towns commissioner.

"Where's Elma?"

"She's on her lunch break and she will back here in an hour."

"Why aren't you on lunch break?"

"I took a 20 minute break an hour before you came in here."

I had an egg sandwich and a glass of milk, that sounds good right about now.

"Why don't you go to the downtown diner and get yourself something good to eat?"

"No," thanks.

"I want to get this done, before I do anything else."

"Are you filing out a Police report?"

"Yes," I am, and I still need to ask you some questions.

"Do you mind if I sit down in this chair over here by the window?"

"Yes," that's fine.

I'm scared of having to be in the Police Station for all this time, you haven't done anything wrong. I trust that you and Virgil are good trustworthy men who follow the law.

"Why aren't you out there with the sheriff?"

"It's my job to protect the Police Station."

"Don't you have a secretary?"

"Yes," I do, her name is Elma.

"Do you get along well with the sheriff?"

"Yes," I do

"May I ask what happened at the crime scene that the sheriff is investigating?"

"I'm not supposed to tell you about that."

All right I'll tell you, but you cannot tell anyone that I told you

"Is that well understood?"

"Yes"

"Last night there was a stabbing at the Hoover residence."

"Did anyone survive?"

"No," the husband and wife were stabbed 30 times in their chests. There dead bodies were found lying face down in the living room.

"Do you know where the killer fled to?"

"No," we don't.

A .22 caliber revolver was lying by the husband's hand. The husband was nicely dressed and so was the wife.

"Any idea when the sheriff's going to find the attacker?"

"No," he's going to search the scene until he finds out which way the killer went.

"Do you or the sheriff know the killers name?"

"No," we don't

Yes, his name is Jozi and this killer has killed 3 people prior to the husband and wife. That's terrible that this Police Department wasn't able to catch him. Yes, but we will catch him.

"When are you going to catch him?"

"As soon as we can."

"What are you going to do with him once you are able to catch him?"

"Charge him with 2 counts of murder and throw him in jail"

I wanted a number of years, hopefully he will be imprisoned for the rest of his pathetic life. I can't stand killers.

"Did you hear that fellows?"

"Yes," we did

I just looked out the window and a pickup truck and compact car just crashed into one another at the intersection. The car must have been traveling at 60 per hour and the truck was only going several miles per hour faster.

"How do you know how fast the vehicles were going?"

"I didn't know; it was just a wild guess."

You both are free to go home, were very busy and can't afford not to get our work done. They both stood up and walked out of the building.

"How are you going to get home?"

"I'll just call a cab."

Eventually both of them found their way back home.

Chapter 4: Turmoil

Meanwhile the twins with chainsaws chased after a hitch hiker, she was absolutely terrified and screamed until they caught up to her and cut her to pieces.

Leaving her cut up and mangled body on the hiking trail to rot. Some hours later, several coyotes came and began to feast on the body. The twins saw this and this angered them.

They fired up their chainsaws and began running after the coyotes. The one twin pulled out a knife and threw it at the coyote, hitting it in the neck.

It yelped, collapsed and soon bled to death. After it collapsed, the twin cut it too pieces. Another hiker came running down the trail, and when he saw the mangled body he immediately ran back to where he came from. Once he was back in his car he dialed 911, and told them what he saw and they sent out an officer.

Him and the officer walked down the trail over to where the body was, he looked at the body trying to figure out the cause of death. The hiker looked at the officer, and said to him this place gives him the creeps.

The Officer took out his phone and called the coroner, the coroner said he could come out in an hour. Meanwhile the twins were cleaning the blood off their chainsaws, in their basement.

A mouse came out of a small hole in the wall, and the one twin saw it and chased after it. While the other twin, was sharpening one of his knives. Eventually the other twin caught up with the mouse and crushed it with his foot, then picked it up and opened the door to the wood stove and threw it in it.

He happened to look down at his apron, and blood was dripping down it. He was also wearing a bulletproof vest, suddenly they heard a commotion outside. They saw two men in white suits, taking the mangled body away.

There were 2 Policemen standing guard, one of them was holding his gun. When out of nowhere a rabid coyote came running out of a thicket, the officer saw it and shot it.

The other people around him angrily said you should've told us before you fired. The other officer asked him what he was going to do with the coyotes body, he replied saying I'll ask if the coroner can take him away.

Both officers walked back to their cars, the one officer walked over to the coroner van. The back doors of it were wide open, and the coroner was placing body parts in a bag. The man looked up and saw the officer standing there, hello officer.

"Could you discard of this coyote for me?"

"I sure will."

This girls body is so mangled, I can't imagine who would do something like this. Her wrist was cut clean off of her body, and even her head was cut off.

Her legs were cut up in several pieces, hopefully this killer will be caught. The detectives will be here in a few minutes, and we'll see what they can dig up. I'm sure that the killer probably made a run for it.

"Do you think there's more than 1 killer?"

"Yes," I do.

"Have you ever heard of the monstrous twins?"

"Yes," I have.

"Do you think they murdered this young girl?"

"No."

This weekend a buddy and I are going to go hunting, I hope that you guys get one, I'm sure that we will. Last year I shot a large buck, it was a trophy buck.

"Do you think a rogue hunter could have murdered this young lady?"

“No.”

I'm done with my responsibilities, so I'm going to head back to the morgue. I'll talk to you later, and the officer walked back to his car and got into it. Suddenly his phone began to ring, he answered the call hello who's this? This is Ben calling from the Fish and Game Commission.

“What are you calling me about?”

“An incident”

Yesterday a hunter called in and said that he had saw a man carrying a chainsaw through the woods. He said that the man was wearing a bloody apron, and there was blood all over him. The man said that he won't go into those woods again.

“Would you mind going through the woods?”

“No,” I wouldn't.

The man saw the chainsaw guy in bower county, 2 weeks ago. The hunter believes that this man is living in the woods, I'll let you know if I find anything and he hung up. He took a sip of his coffee, and opened his lunch pail and took out an apple. He took a bite out of it and put it down on the console and got out of his car.

He walked out of the parking lot and into the woods, he saw the detectives gathering their stuff to leave. One of them walked over to him, I'm glad to be leaving these woods, you'll never find me in the woods after dark.

"What did you discover?"

"Foot prints, and there were drag marks on the ground that led deeper into the woods."

"We found a bag of beef jerky, and an old rusty chainsaw chain."

"Where are you gentlemen off to next?"

"Another crime scene."

"How many crime scenes do you go to in a day?"

"Four of them."

It's been nice talking with you Sir, but I have to go now bye. Many thoughts were going through the officers mind. He thought to himself I hope they can find this crazy man. He walked past the twins home, they watched him from the window.

"Should we kill him now or wait?"

"Wait."

Wait until he gets deeper into the woods, I've never liked the Lawmen.

"Where are we going to discard his body?"

"In the ravine."

"What are we going to do with his gun?"

"Keep it."

A hunter came walking down the trail, with his rifle over his shoulder. If he comes any closer I'm going to kill him, then he may shoot you not if I'm quick enough.

You can't start your chainsaw yet, wait until he gets closer to us or it may spook him. He walked over to their house and knocked on the door, the door immediately swung open catching him by surprise.

He had no time to escape, the twins came running at him with their chainsaws. He punched 1 of them, but it only enraged them. They cut off his arm, blood spewed out everywhere and the man collapsed. The twins got into a cutting frenzy, and cut apart his body.

"Do you think his buddies are going to come look for him?"

"Yes," I do.

You and I should leave this house and hide out in the woods, by the ravine. You realize that the law is going to come knocking soon at our door, I don't want them to catch us.

There's already one officer walking around the woods, I'm sure that there are more coming today. I'm getting hungry and our refrigerator is empty, I don't mind eating a person but you do. I'm tired of waiting here, let's go after the officer now.

"Where are you going?"

"Inside to fill up my chainsaw with gas."

After filling up his chainsaw, he left the basement. It's time for us to play hide and seek with the officer, we're going to cut him to pieces. We're not just going to run out at him, but sneak up on him. I don't want us getting shot, we're going to live a long time.

"Have you tightened your chain lately?"

"No," I haven't.

"Where do you think we'll find more people to terrorize?"

"At the campground."

"I think you're more evil than I am."

"Do you remember where our bunker is back here?"

"Yes," I do.

I have a feeling that we're getting close to where the officer is, we must speak softer. Look at all of those trees that have fallen down over there, we should chop one of them up for firewood. No, I'd rather cut up people instead, you're such a monster. Quick get down there's comes a helicopter, I doubt he's looking for us.

That was sure a waste of our time, I'm mad that this officer is on our land. I wonder where that loud music is coming from, it's coming from the campground.

That's where were going to go next, then a lot of people are going to see us. I know that our faces are deformed, and our looks will scare a lot of people. They soon came upon the officer, who was wondering aimlessly through the woods.

Don't get up yet stay behind the tree stump with me, we'll strike when he gets closer to us. I don't think this officer is so smart, he'll be an easy target for us, he's coming this way get ready. I know what you're going to say but I have no problem with killing him.

One of them jumped up, and struck the officer in the head with his chainsaw, knocking him to the ground. They both fired up their chainsaws, the officer's face was bloodied and he was barely breathing. Let's take this officer out of his misery, if you don't make the first move I will.

I'll give you one more minute to make him move then I'm going to cut him up like you should have. The evil twin, began cutting up the officer's body. You can now cut in, if you'd like.

He cut into the man's torso, and went on to cut off his foot. We should have brought a bag with us to put his body parts in, I don't know about you but I don't mind carrying his body over to the ravine.

Once they got to the top of the ravine, they threw his body down the ravine, followed by his body parts. Don't tell me that you feel bad for that man.

Your mask is about to fall off your face, I will have to check it then. I have far more blood on me than you do. After we're done terrorizing the campground we're going to head back to our bunker.

We should steal the officer's car, we can't now because the keys were in his shirt pocket and that's in the ravine.

"Did you see that camera on the tree?"

"No," I didn't.

"Who do you think is watching us through that?"

"No, it just takes pictures."

Once you figure out how to get it off the tree I'll cut it up, it's strapped on so well that I can't make it budge. His evil twin fired up his chainsaw, and cut the trail cam a part. I don't like this tree either I'm going to cut it down, you're cutting down everything today. Eventually they reached the campground, they hid behind an old rusty truck.

There were several young couples, who were sitting by the fire having a conversation. There was 1 boy, he was chasing after a squirrel. Don't go running away too far from here, you don't know what could be in those woods. I know that you wanted to play with that new kite that we got you but it's too windy, put a smile on your face.

I know that you don't like listening to us talk, but we're enjoying ourselves. Play with this bouncy ball, but don't throw it too far. Mom we should have brought our dog with, we will next time. I'll be keeping an eye on you while you're playing, don't worry we won't be here much longer.

I want to talk to dad though, you can talk to him later. Suddenly the sound of thunder erupted, and this scared the boy causing him to run over to his mother.

Who was getting something out of the trunk. He hugged his mother's leg tightly, It's going to be okay it's only thunder. Mom I'm still scared, I want to sit inside the car.

Go ahead the doors are open, once he got inside he lowered the windows a little bit. He let out a yawn, it's okay if you're tired you can sleep, I'll be back soon with your dad. The little boy picked up his stuffed dragon, and cuddled with it. He soon went off to sleep.

His mother walked over to her husband, I'm sorry to interrupt but I have a bad feeling. I think that we're being watched. I think that you had too many drinks, I don't think so.

Chapter 5: Miss Fortune & Uncertainty

We need to think about getting out of here, and just leave our friends behind. You're embarrassing us in front of them, I don't care. It's clouding up it's going to rain soon, I just felt a drop.

"Are you the rain forecaster now?"

"No," I'm not.

This is no laughing matter, but serious. She took his beer and placed it on the ground, I was drinking that you know. You haven't been in this kind of mood for a while.

I want to at least finish my beer, no you've had enough. I've watched you drink down 3 beers now, you're losing control of yourself. I don't think so, I know how to handle myself.

"Do you guys see what she's doing to me?"

"Yes," we do.

We aren't going to speak for you, you're on your own. If you keep it up your friends are going to walk away from you, I don't think they would do that. You and your friends can do whatever you want, I'm getting in the car and taking our child home. Please let me have the car keys, fine take them.

You know that I don't like fighting with you, you just get this way when you drink. If you push me, that would be the last thing that you would do. If you say one more thing I'm not going to come back later and pick you up, you're going to break your own back.

"Aren't you going to hug me?"

"No," you don't deserve it.

She rolled her eyes at him and walked back to the car, wake up were going home.

"Mom what's going on?"

"Your dad's in a bad mood again."

I thought that we were going to the grocery store on our way back. No we aren't going there I changed my mind, I'm sorry but I'm just short on patience right now. We'll go get some ice cream tomorrow, I hope that's alright with you. Your dad can stay there until the cows come home, soon they got home.

The Twins fired up there chainsaws, the people in the campground began to look around. One of the couples took shelter in there RV, while everyone else stayed sitting.

The twins came running out, the people saw them and scattered. The girls were screaming and running for their lives, one of the men ran over to his car and pulled out a bat from the trunk.

He swung at one of them, but was quickly overpowered. The blade went deep into his arm, he yelled out in agony. He tried to get away but the twin whacked him in the back with his chainsaw, once he was down, the twin put the chainsaw blade right through his back.

The man's body laid there motionless, the twins chased after their next victim, a girl was trying to get in her car. Both twins ran at her, she tried to run but tripped over something and fell onto her back and screamed.

The one twin kicked her in the head, knocking her out. They sawed her in half, then walked over to the RV. The couple who were inside were huddled up together, one of them called the Police. The evil twin smashed out the window, and tried to gain entry but failed.

While the other twin was sawing into the door, trying to cut it off its hinges. The evil twin came over and helped with cutting the door out, after a while the door fell down.

The twins entered the RV, and wreaked havoc on the couple killing them in a matter of minutes. An officer drove down the muddy path until he reached the campground, once he got out of his car he saw the mangled bodies lying there, he froze for a moment.

The very sight of the bodies made him nauseous, he carefully approached the RV. He could hear chainsaws running, and fired 1 round at the RV. Out of nowhere someone threw a knife at him, hitting him in the arm. He yelled out whomever threw that knife is under arrest, you have injured an officer.

You better come out here with your arms up, I'm only going to give you five minutes to come out or I'm going in there. The officer left the knife in, when the officer came running over to enter the RV.

The evil twin was standing behind where the door used to be, and when the officer entered, before he could make a move his head was sawed clean off.

We better get out of here now, this place will be crawling with Police soon. The twins quickly made their way back to the woods, eventually they reached their bunker.

They opened the door to the bunker, and entered it. The local Police Department couldn't get ahold of the officer, so they sent out another officer. It didn't take this officer long to get to the scene, he was horrified by the mangled bodies, but kept his composure. He took a walk around the campground, then walked over to the RV.

His jaw dropped when he seen the headless officers body lying there. He noticed that there was a knife in his arm, he pulled the knife out of his arm and pulled out an evidence baggie out of his pocket and put the knife into it.

He entered the RV, and was surprised to find more mangled up bodies. He quickly exited the RV, and ran back to his car. He got in his car and placed the evidence baggie on the dash, then he called base, a woman answered hello Officer Jeff. I'm calling you to let you know that we have an officer down.

We won't be needing the paramedics, the officer is in pieces. I found a knife in the dead officers arm, I'm hoping that we'll be able to find fingerprints on that knife to find out whomever it belonged to. I'm not going to stick around unless you let me call for backup.

I'll let you call for backup, you're busy I'll let you go. He immediately called for backup, we have an officer down. 2 officers are on en route to your location, they should be there in minutes.

"Is there an active shooter there?"

"No," there's not.

Some kind of massacre must have happened here, and the fugitive is probably on foot. There's a chance that he's hiding out in the woods. He said goodbye and hung up the radio, suddenly a man came frantically running over to him.

"Where did you come from Sir?"

"I came from 100 yards that way, I was hiding under my car."

"Did you happen to see what happened?"

"Yes," I did.

You're shaking awful a lot, it's okay because I'm here. There were 2 of them and they were carrying chainsaws, I didn't get a good look at their faces.

"Where did they come from?"

"They came from behind that old truck over there."

"Did they say anything?"

"No."

I'm still not comfortable with being here at the moment, I'm afraid that they're going to come back.

"Did you see them kill the officer?"

"No," I didn't.

I was so scared that I almost fainted, if they come out again I'm going to shoot them both. Eventually backup arrived, they walked over to the officer already at the scene. I'm glad to be seeing you boys now, this man standing beside me survived the attack.

"How long have these bodies been lying around here?"

"They've been here since I pulled in."

It's only right that these bodies are given a proper burial, I'm going to call the coroner. After you make that call, I want you to make a call to the sheriff and tell him that we need to do an all-out manhunt today.

The sooner they're found the safer everyone will be. Also tell him, to bring out surveillance drones, I'll do that. If the sheriff has any more questions I'll just bring my phone over to you.

"What would you like me to do?"

"Stand guard here, until I think of something for you to do."

After the manhunt is over we're going to hold a special ceremony for the fallen officer. I hate to say it but I think we're going to be looking for these 2 fugitives for a while before we find them. I think with the surveillance drones, we'll find them much faster.

"Where are you going?"

"To see if there's any cut up bodies near the old truck, let us know if you find anything."

The man ran over to the old truck, and all he could find were the fugitives footprints all around it. He walked into the woods, but kept an eye out for the fugitives. He noticed that there was a tree cut down, and went deeper into the woods.

Sometime later he came to a house, he walked up to the house and knocked on the door but there was no answer. He said hello is anyone here, and no one came out. He walked around to the back of the place and noticed that the basement door was left open.

He thought to himself this maybe somekind of trap, and stood there thinking about it. Against his better judgment he entered it anyway, there was blood covering the floor.

The lights above him were flickering, there were dead mice lying there on a table. There was an old chainsaw hanging up in the back of the basement, behind the table was a large jar. He picked up the jar and what he seen in it, left him horrified. It was someone's head, and it was missing its eyes.

He carefully put the jar back, he wasn't sure what he might come across next. The hairs on the back of his head and arms were standing up, he thought to himself I hope that the homeowners don't catch me. At the bottom of the steps there was a deer carcass, its legs were missing and so was it's head.

He walked into a cobweb, there was an old radio sitting in the corner. He thought that he heard footsteps above him, and quickly found his way out of the basement. Several crows came flying overhead squawking up a storm, and one of them landed on the branch of a tree nearby.

Get out of here you annoying crow, you don't scare me. He reached down and picked up a rock, and threw it at the upstairs window. He could see the curtains moving, he wasn't sure what to expect next.

He could hear something shuffling around inside the house, he quickly ran from the house, and hid behind a big tree. He thought to himself there must be something living up in that one bedroom, a few minutes later something broke through the window and climbed down from the roof.

The creature was all black with no hair, and walked on all fours, with glowing eyes. It was missing one of its ears, and had a scar on its side. It was now closing in on him, he thought to himself just let this nightmare go away. While It was looking the other way he made a run for it, he ducked behind another tree.

To his relief the creature wasn't following him, once again he ran and soon was out of the woods. He feverishly ran over to the officers, your all in danger get in your vehicles right now. The officers stopped what they were doing and got into their vehicles, the man got into the officers car.

"What was chasing you?"

"Some kind of creature."

It should be here any minute now, thanks for letting me know. I found a house in the middle of the woods, and the basement door was open so I entered the place. My curiosity got the best of me so I wandered around the basement, and the things that I saw horrified me.

"What was in the basement?"

"A deer carcass, and someone's head in a jar."

Believe me you don't want to go into that house now, not with that creature running around yet.

"Do you think shooting the creature would kill it?"

"Yes," I do.

The creature resembles a black panther, I see it, it's coming our way now. It's coming over to your side now, and it jumped up on the window letting out a growl. You better shoot that thing before it breaks through the window and grabs you, I'll shoot it before that happens.

While you were in the woods I got a call from the sheriff, and he'll be out here in 1 hour. We have to take care of this creature before he gets here, you're being awfully laxed. I would have pulled out my gun and shot that thing by now, besides that it's probably harassing the other officers right now.

"Are you going to make other officers do it?"

"No," then don't be lazy.

The officer swung open the door, and waited for the creature to come over. He shouted out, I'm here come and get me. The creature turned towards him, and came running right for him. He shot it 2 times, and it collapsed, he walked over to it and without warning it brought its head up.

He quickly backed up from it, he shot it 1 more time then he returned to his car. That creature just won't stay down, if I wasn't watching that thing it would have bit my leg.

"Can you see what the creature is doing now?"

"Yes," it's not moving.

The 2 other officers came walking over to the car, he rolled down the window.

"Did you hit what you were shooting at?"

"Yes," it's lying over there.

Both officers walked over to the creature, that thing is awfully horrible looking. This thing is missing some of its skin, and its tail is barely attached.

After seeing this thing I won't be walking my dog at night, anymore. I swear that I just saw it's chest moving, you better be kidding me. If this thing isn't dead it's a zombie, look there it goes again.

"Now do you see what I mean?"

"Yes," I do.

If you're not going to shoot it I will, the other officer took out his gun and quickly shot it. You should have shot it in the head, I will if it moves again. I don't think whatever this is comes from our planet, I'd have to agree with you on that.

This creature sure has big teeth, and odd shaped eyes. I don't think this thing is a canine, but I could be wrong. I wouldn't touch it if I were you, I just wanted to feel what its fur felt like. This creature's fur could be contaminated, I don't believe that.

Chapter 6: Winning The Battle

They got tired of looking at the creature and walked back to their cars. The officer and the man said look at both of those officers they sure have spent awhile looking at that creature, I wonder what made that officer shoot it again. He could have been afraid of it, maybe but I don't think that's the reason.

The man saw that there was a white box sitting on the center console, he opened it up and found donuts. I see that you found my donut stash, go ahead you can have one. There's plenty of different flavors here, the man reached in and took out a donut.

That's my favorite kind of donut too, you and I are a lot alike. If you weren't here, I'd be busy texting on my phone. I prefer calling people over texting them, that's where you differ from me.

"Do you have extra water somewhere in your car?"

"Yes," I do.

Don't worry I have plenty of water in this car for you and I. The man stayed in the car, while the officer went out to stretch his legs. He was alarmed when he saw that the creature was no longer lying there.

He quickly unholstered his gun, he looked over and saw that the creature was retreating back to the woods. He followed the creature, it looked back at him and snarled. I'm going to get you no matter what, he heard something off in the distance and hid behind a tree stump.

He looked over and saw two men coming up out from a bunker wielding chainsaws. The creature ran over to the twins and stood beside them, one of the men put his hand down and patted the creature on the head.

The officer thought to himself now I know who this creature belongs to, the two men headed towards him. He stood up, and the two men immediately spotted him. Hello fellas, someone told me that you both were causing a lot of trouble at the campground.

You're both wanted for murder, the both of them fired up their chainsaws and came right for him. He fired one bullet at them, before getting sawed up. He was dead before he knew what happened to him, we just killed another officer, his evil twin mumbled whatever.

"What are we going do with his body?"

"Let the zombie cat eat him."

"How many of our zombie cats are living in the underground tunnels?"

"Thirty of them."

We can't be standing out in the open anymore, so they retreated back into the bunker. We should go down into the tunnels and check on the cats, I'm sure that they miss seeing us.

I doubt that they can even see us anymore, I'm hoping that those twenty deer carcasses that we've fed to them was enough food for them, I'm sure that it was.

"Have you figured out a way yet to make the cats stronger?"

"Yes," I have.

I found a can labeled biohazard, and I threw that down into the tunnel. You're being a mad scientist, his evil twin rolled his eyes at him. You realize that the army may come looking for us, it will be difficult for them to find us. When I'm done beefing these cats up not even a grenade will stop them.

When they got down into the tunnel, the cats were devouring the deer carcass. You see the cats still recognize us, that cat laying over there is bigger than all the rest of them. There must have been growth hormone in that can't too, I'll call that one the Goliath cat.

"How long ago did you start breeding the cats?"

"Two years ago."

I'm spent some time down here with them doing experiments with them, they're very sensitive to vibrations and can smell blood far away.

"How's they're hearing?"

"It's good."

"Did you the lock entrance door?"

"Yes," I did.

"Do you remember when we killed the pipeline surveyor?"

"Yes," I do.

"What about it?"

"I read the papers in the binder that the surveyor had."

On one of the papers that I read it said that they're going to be burrowing tunnels to make the pipeline. I'm pretty sure that they're going to start it tomorrow, don't worry if they drill into our tunnels our cats will take care of them.

If the cats fail to take care of them then we'll will cut them up. Meanwhile, the 2 officer's were wondering what had happened to the man, and the officer. I think that one of us better go looking for the officer and the man, I'm not stepping a foot in those woods. In another five minutes the sheriff will be here, along with his fugitive search team.

If you and I go in those woods and go missing, he'll look for us instead of the fugitive. There comes the sheriff now, followed by the search team. The sheriff pulled in beside them, and quickly got out of his truck. He came walking over to them with a stern look on his face. The officers quickly got out of their car and greeted him.

One of the officers is on the ground without his head, and another one of the officers went missing in the woods over there over an hour ago, and the victim of the attack earlier is missing too. The search team is currently getting their drones ready, the drones will only be able to fly for half an hour.

"Did the drones replace the search dogs?"

"Yes," they have.

I think that was a bad move, the dogs can sniff out people, the drones can't do that. The Police Enrichment Board President mentioned that we should have done that, you shouldn't have listened to him. Neither one of us listen to him, and you shouldn't either.

We've been thinking about what happened to the deputy Ross, I'd like to hear this, this ought to be good. We believe that he was murdered, by a rogue officer, on his way to work.

"Can you tell me the name of that officer?"

"Yes," we can.

"He's no longer working for the force"

"I understand that but what's his name?"

"Officer Keven Blix."

"Do either one of you have a clue where he lives?"

"No," we don't.

"How's your dog doing?"

"The sheriff replied he's doing good thanks."

Yesterday you were telling me that a tree fell, at your residence. It was a pretty big tree, and took me awhile to cut up. I called Herman logging to remove several more trees from my property, they weren't overly expensive.

That's a good thing but I don't need any trees removed, I cut down all the trees around my place a long time ago. It's been nice talking to the both of you, I'll be back over once I'm done with my business.

It's windier out here than what we have expected, we might have to wait ten minutes to fly these drones. We don't have that kind of time, if we wait around like that we'll never find the fugitive. Every one of you knows how I don't have much patience.

"What's in that silver case?"

"A new type of drone."

You can gladly take it out and look at it, it's a new law enforcement drone. It has a tazor gun fastened to it, I've never seen such a thing before. The tazor gun is twice as powerful, I have something else to show you too.

Hold on a minute, let me get it out of the back of my truck. He eventually got it out of his truck, that's larger than I thought it was. That thing resembles a giant worm, this is called the bunker searcher.

"What's it made out of?"

"Steel."

It borrows through the ground with ease, it can go 40 miles per hour.

"Does it run off of a battery?"

"No," it don't.

It has a gasoline engine, and can run for several hours before needing to be filled up.

"What happens when it finds a bunker?"

"It will alert me on the app."

"Can I see the app?"

"Yes," you can.

He quickly brought out his phone, and brought up the app. I like how it shows where it is on the map, and it shows you how much fuel is left in it's gas tank.

"How do you turn this thing on?"

"Just push in the push start and the away it goes."

"Would you mind if I started it?"

"No," I wouldn't.

I don't see any push start button, that's because you have to lift up this rubber cap to get to it. He lifted up the rubber cap and there the button was, and pressed it in. The bunker searcher started up and took off, into the ground. That thing didn't waste any time getting started.

"Will it let you know if it doesn't find anything?"

"Yes," it will.

This is one smart robot, I can't imagine how much it cost.

"Can I buy one of these things?"

"No," it's still a prototype.

"How many times have you used this thing?"

"Several times"

"How much longer until I can buy one?"

"2 months."

Since the wind has died down, let me go ahead and start flying the drone. Then the sheriff walked over to the leader of the search team, and gave him the okay to start looking for the fugitive on foot.

"How far away from here can you fly that drone?"

"6 miles."

We have the antenna extension on it already, that must have been expensive. You'd be surprised it wasn't overly expensive, I'll gladly let you control this thing. No, thanks I'd probably crash it.

"Is this drone made in this country?"

"No," it's not.

"How long do you think they're be looking on foot for the suspect?"

"For three hours."

An hour quickly went by and the app on the other man's phone went off. He gestured for the sheriff to come over to him, the app's showing me that the bunker is in the middle of the woods.

"Does it say the deph of the bunker?"

"Yes."

The blue number in the upper left hand corner is the depth of the bunker, and this red number is how many minutes it's been underground.

"Must you go retrieve it yourself when it's done searching?"

"No," I just hit a button that says come back.

Whoever made this thing thought of it all, the screen on my phone just went blank. My phone don't normally act like this, I wonder what's going on with it. I'll just reset it and see what happens. Suddenly there was an explosion, whatever it was it blew up in the woods.

I just opened up the app again and it's saying that it had an error, then it was the bunker searcher that blew up. I hope none of the searchers out there got injured from it, hopefully you're right.

Let's you and I take a walk over there, they walked through the woods until they came to where they thought the bunker was. I just found the door that leads down into the bunker, I'm not so sure you should open that.

"Why?"

"Because the fugitive could be down there pointing a gun up at us."

The doors locked so we can't open it anyway. Meanwhile under the ground, the blast was so powerful that it blew up the twins and killed the zombie cats, then the tunnels collapsed in on them.

The sheriff and the search team searched until 6:00 that night then quit their search. The Sheriff went back to the Police Station, and wrote up an report of what had happened, and soon afterwards headed home.